This book ~~belongs to:~~
is shared with

_____

_____

_____

the tree of goodness

to all who doubt

© 2016 Conscious Stories LLC

Illustrations by Marcel Marais
Character Design by
Miguel Gamez-Cuevas

Published by
Conscious Stories LLC
4800 Baseline Rd,
Suite E104-365
Boulder, CO
80303
USA

www.consciousstories.com

First Edition
Library of Congress
Control Number: 2017902515
ISBN 978-1-943750-11-5

Printed in China

1 2 3 4 5 6 7 8 9 10

The last 20 minutes of every day are precious.

Dear parents, teachers, and readers,

This story has been gift-wrapped with two simple mindfulness
practices to help you connect more deeply with your children in
the last 20 minutes of each day.

● Quietly set your intention for calm, open connection.

● Then start your story time with the **Snuggle Breathing
Meditation**. Read each line aloud and take slow, deep breaths
together in order to relax and be present.

● At the end of the story, you will find **The Goodness Stretch**.
This will help you and your child reconnect with the goodness in
every cell of your bodies.

Enjoy snuggling into togetherness!

Andrew

An easy breathing meditation

Snuggle Breathing

Our story begins with us breathing together.
Say each line aloud and then
take a slow deep breath in and out.

I breathe for me

I breathe for you

I breathe for us

I breathe for all that surrounds us

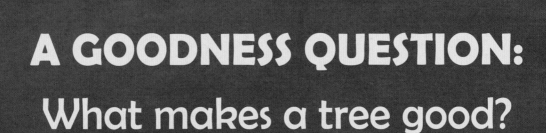

A GOODNESS QUESTION:

What makes a tree good?

Is a tree good
because it makes us wood
or shade to enjoy a picnic?

Is a tree good
because it makes a chair
where we can rest our derriéres?

Is a tree good
because it makes us fire
that warms and cooks
when we tire?

No, that's not what makes a tree good.

A tree is made out of good.
It starts as a seed,
sprouts tiny roots, branches,
and leaves.

good

good

good

15

The good becomes wood that grows tall or bends, standing alone or with a few friends.

Sometimes it's leafy
or knotted with bumps.
Often it kinks and has a
few lumps.

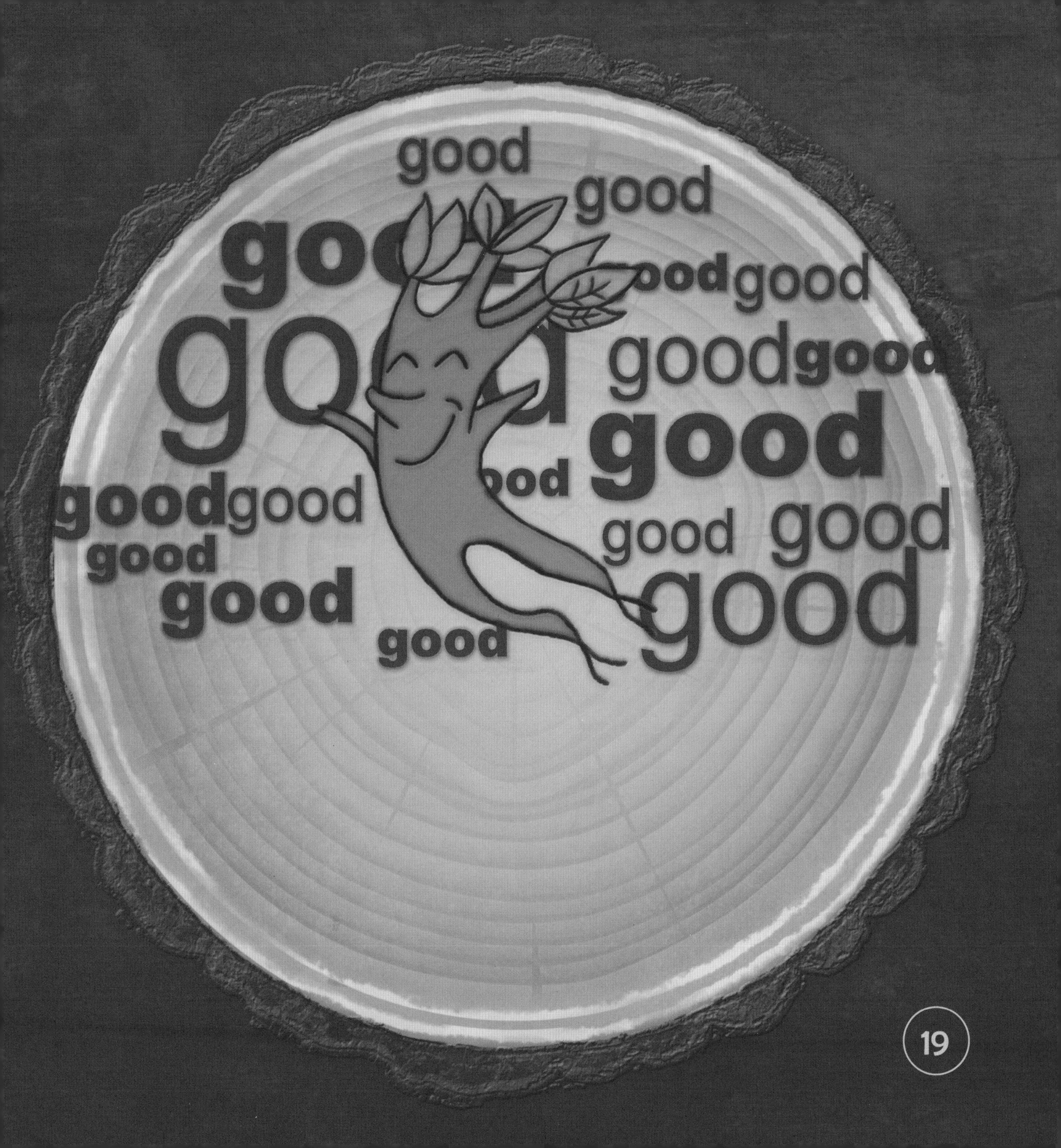

But that's OK.

A tree is good
without any reason,
flowers or leaves,
no matter the season.

A tree is good
with no work at all.
It's already good
short or tall.

What makes a tree good?
The answer is this:
A tree is good
just how it is.

Stand in your goodness.

Make this stretch your bedtime reminder that every cell in your body is made of goodness.

Relaxing your body

The Goodness Stretch

Plant your feet on the ground.

1

Feel roots stretching out of your feet into the earth.

2

Stretch your arms like branches to the sky.

3

Close your eyes and
connect with goodness.

5

Feel your trunk tall
and strong.

4

good
good

Smile.

6

7 Take 3 deep
breaths before
going to sleep.

29

the collection

The Conscious Bedtime Story Club

snuggling into togetherness

the prayer who searched for God

Andrew Newman
Illustrated by Alexis Aronson

the fish who searched for water

the bee who could not choose her flower

Andrew Newman
Illustrated by Marcella Marais

the dad who didn't know

the hug who got stuck

Andrew

the forgetful elephant

Andrew Newman

the laughing witch

Andrew Newman

a little light

Andrew Newman
Illustrated by Rocio Belyssi

the elephant who tried to tiptoe

how diablo became Spirit

Andrew Newman
& Anna Breytenbach
Illustrated by Alexis Aronson

the boy who searched for silence

Andrew Newman
Illustrated by Alexis Aronson

the tree of goodness

Andrew Newman
Illustrated by Marcella Marais

what the club offers

A collection of stories with wise and lovable characters who teach spiritual values to your children

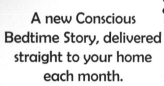

A new Conscious Bedtime Story, delivered straight to your home each month.

One whole year of bedtime stories

Meet wonderful, heroic characters with big hearts and deep values as they encounter exciting challenges and move toward freedom.

Simple mindfulness practices

Enjoy easy breathing practices that soften the atmosphere and create deep connection when reading together.

Create your own story books

Unleash your creativity by writing and coloring your own stories.

Reflective activity pages

Cherish open sharing time with your children at the end of each day.

Delivered to your home

Make one decision today, and experience a whole year of delightful stories.

Supportive parenting community

Join a community of conscious parents who seek connection with their children.

Download your free coloring book from
www.consciousstories.com

31

Andrew Newman - author

Andrew Newman has followed his deep longing for connection and his passion for spiritual development in a 12 year-long study of healing. He is a graduate of the Barbara Brennan School of Healing and a qualified Non-dual Kabbalistic healer. He has been actively involved in men's work through the Mankind Project since 2006.

In addition to his therapy practice, Andrew has published over 1,500 donated poems as the PoemCatcher, served as a volunteer coordinator for Habitat for Humanity in South Africa, and directed Edinburgh's Festival of Spirituality and Peace.

Marcelle Marais - illustrator

Marcelle Marais is an illustrator and animator born in South Africa, with 10 years experience working on a variety of projects from music videos and illustrating books to supplying the local and international advertising industry. He resides near the ocean and has a love for nature, art, literature, and anything aquatic.

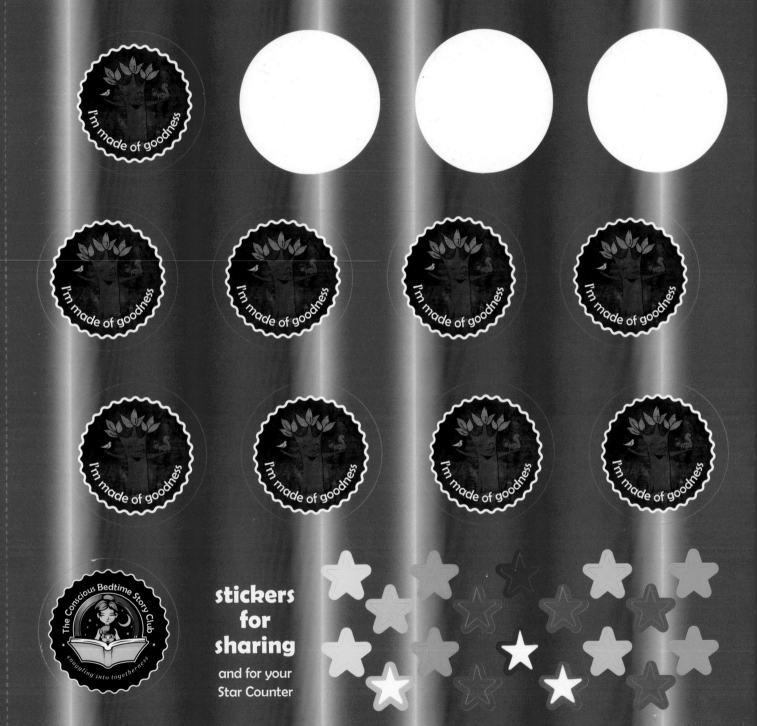

I'm made of goodness

stickers
for
sharing
and for your
Star Counter

The Conscious Bedtime Story Club
snuggling into togetherness

Star Counter

Every time you breathe together and
read aloud, you make a star shine in the
night sky.

Place a sticker, or color in a star, to count
how many times you have read this book.